Jake

the Good Bad Dog

Written by Annette Butterworth
Illustrated by Nick Butterworth

Catnip Publishing
HAPPY CAT BOOKS

Chapter One

Jake was a bad dog. He knew he was. Sometimes he tried to be good but it was no use.

He loved to chase the ducks in the park. He would sneak up behind them when they were dozing. Then he would bark loudly and watch, as they rushed for the safety of the lake, complaining noisily.

Jake couldn't resist the smell of the dirty washing. Whenever it was being sorted out, he just had to play with it. Then he would leave it lying all over the house.

He had to roll in the sheep's droppings on the common. He liked the smell. Besides, he needed to smell like a sheep if he was going to creep up on them and round them up.

Then there was food. Or more particularly, chocolate. No chocolate was safe if Jake could reach it. Once he ate fourteen chocolate cream eggs, one after the other. He was sorry afterwards, especially as they made him ill, but he just couldn't resist them.

He couldn't help being bad.

Of course, Jake wanted to be good. He would have liked to be like those clever dogs he saw on the television. He did try to do as he was told, but it was so difficult when there always seemed to be something that needed to be chased or ripped or chewed.

He wanted to be like Holly, the dog who lived next door. Holly was Jake's friend. She was a Rough Collie, like Lassie. She was good and she was also very beautiful. Holly had even been to Crufts.

Crufts! The biggest and best dog show in the world! Of all the reasons to be good, this was surely the most important. Only the best dogs went to Crufts. Holly had told Jake all about it. It sounded like heaven.

Crufts! Even the name sounded like a delicious kind of dog biscuit. Jake longed to see Crufts for himself. He wasn't really sure what it was like, but he thought there must be lots of chocolate there. Perhaps it was made of chocolate. Really heavenly!

Holly had told Jake how exciting it was to visit Crufts. Wonderful smells! Large halls with banners hanging from the ceilings and wide green carpet everywhere, perfect for rolling on. In the middle, a big open space called the Main Ring, where the clever dogs would show off their agility and obedience tricks. The top dogs gathered in the Main

Ring to decide who was the best of the lot.

Holly said to Jake that she would love to be chosen one day, but was sure she wasn't good enough. Jake was very sure she was good enough, and loyally, and loudly, told her so.

Jake liked the sound of all the different stands with lots of food on them, especially the free samples that Holly talked about!

But most of all, Jake loved to hear about all the dogs. Thousands of them, according to Holly. All different shapes and sizes from all over the world. Australia, America, Alaska even, France, Germany, Belgium. Belgium. Jake thought his grandad came from Belgium and he liked the idea of meeting his long lost relatives.

Holly had met one dog from Alaska. She didn't know where Alaska was but she thought it must be cold because the dog had a huge thick coat of fur and said that his father used to pull a sledge.

All this talk of Crufts made Jake very excited. He told Holly he would go with her next year on her wonderful visit to Crufts.

But Jake was in for a disappointment. Sadly, Holly told Jake that a dog has to be a pedigree and specially chosen to go to Crufts. The only other dogs there are the very clever ones in the obedience competition. Holly gently told Jake that he would not be allowed into Crufts.

Charles, the Irish Wolfhound who lived on the other side of Jake's garden, laughed. Of course they wouldn't let riffraff like Jake into Crufts. It was unusual for Charles to bring himself to speak to Jake at all, because

Charles thought himself very grand. His father had been the mascot for a regiment in the British Army and had told Charles not to mix with riffraff. To Charles, a mongrel like Jake was riffraff. Charles spent his time ignoring Jake's efforts to be friends.

But if Jake wasn't good, he wasn't stupid. There were lots of things that he could do. He could let himself in from the garden, for instance. He would simply jump up at the door handle and pull it down. The door would swing open and in he would go. But instead of his owners, Mr and Mrs Foster, being pleased, they were more likely to shout at Jake for scratching the door.

In the summer time, when one of the upstairs windows was open, Jake could hang out of it and see right to the end of the street. He thought he was very clever but even Jake had to admit, it wasn't clever enough for Crufts.

One of his best tricks was to pick up a big balloon without bursting it. It had taken him a long time to work this out, but one Christmas, when there'd been lots of balloons left lying about the floor, he'd had plenty to practise on. After he'd burst eleven of them, he discovered that he could pick them up from one end by the knot.

Jake proudly walked around with one for quite some time before he received the applause he was after. Then his owners found the other burst balloons. And once again he was told off.

So Jake knew he wasn't good. He'd certainly been told enough times. The Crufts obedience competition was just out of the question. And, although he did think that he was quite handsome, he knew he wasn't a pedigree.

Jake had to accept that the one thing he wanted more than anything else, to go to Crufts, would never happen.

Chapter Two

At the bottom of Jake's garden, there was a gap in the hedge that he could squeeze through. On the other side, there lay an overgrown wilderness of a garden, which, to Jake, was the only kind of garden worth having. One corner of this garden that he particularly liked had a pond with frogs in it. Jake liked to wait by the pond until the frogs started jumping. Then he would startle them by leaping on them and chasing them. Jake thought this was a terrific game. The frogs weren't so sure.

It was in the middle of one of these games that Jake met Sam. Since then, Sam had become Jake's favourite person.

Sam lived in a ramshackle house that stood in the wilderness of a garden. He was no longer a young man. He'd moved to England a long time ago from his home in Belgium. Unfortunately, he had always found it difficult to speak English and he had very few friends and no relations in England. He was a lonely man.

Until he met Jake.

Sam understood Jake and Jake understood Sam. Sam knew that Jake was a loyal dog who had unusual abilities. Jake knew that Sam was a kind man who didn't mind where he dug in the garden and would always share his sandwiches. Jake loved the smell of Sam. It reminded him of the dirty washing he liked to play with. It pleased Jake that Sam was from Belgium. Maybe Sam knew his grandad. Jake and Sam became firm friends. Sam asked Mr and Mrs Foster if he could take Jake for walks, and now it was nearly always Sam who took Jake out.

One morning Jake squeezed through the hedge to find Sam sitting outside, feeding the birds. Jake knew he had to be very quiet until Sam had finished. Sam didn't like the birds to be frightened. Jake wanted to chase them off but he kept still for Sam.

When the birds had gone, he moved up to sit next to Sam and nuzzled at his hand. Jake was feeling very disappointed this morning because Holly had told him that

her owners had entered her again in the
Crufts competition. He would have loved
to watch her there.

"Hallo, old boy," said Sam to Jake. "How
you doing? You don't seem to be your old
bouncy self this morning. Tell you what,
Sam will take you for a
nice walk."

Sam could always
talk more easily
to Jake because
he didn't worry
about how
he sounded.

Jake's ears pricked up at the suggestion of a walk. Their favourite park was only five minutes away. Soon Sam and Jake were walking through the big, green, park gates.

Jake rushed everywhere, checking up on things. There were a few squirrels who needed chasing up a tree and some ducks that needed putting in their place. Sam let him get on with it: he knew Jake didn't mean any harm. The animals were used to him.

They made their way through the park until they came to the football pitch where Jake began to nuzzle at an old carrier bag that Sam was carrying.

"All right, boy, steady on. I know what you want. Give me a chance!" Sam reached into the bag and pulled out a football that he always brought with him.

"O.K. Jake. Let's have a game."

At the sight of the ball, Jake leapt into the air and ran round and round in circles until the game began.

Jake was really marvellous with a football. He dribbled the ball back to Sam right from the other end of the pitch. Sam kicked the ball into the air and Jake headed it a few times with his long muzzle. Then he trapped it with his front legs and dribbled it back with his nose.

As Jake got more excited, he crept closer and closer as Sam was trying to kick the ball. Sam shouted, "Ten yards! Ten yards!" and Jake backed away until Sam was satisfied he was far enough away not to get kicked.

People would often gather to watch Sam and Jake. They were amazed that a dog could be so clever with a ball. Sadly for Jake, even being able to play football didn't qualify a dog for Crufts.

Today, there was a football match being played on the pitch next to Jake and Sam's. Before Sam realised it, Jake had disappeared.

"Where has he gone?" thought Sam.

Suddenly, Sam looked across at the football pitch next to him and saw Jake right in the middle of it! He'd decided to join in a proper game of football. Jake was rushing along the pitch, nudging the football with his muzzle and beating everybody in sight. Both teams of footballers chased after him but nobody was quick enough to catch Jake.

He rushed around the pitch, causing havoc and was enjoying himself so much that he didn't hear Sam's frantic shouts to come back and leave the ball.

One after the other, the footballers tried to get their ball back. It was no use. Jake was too quick and the pitch too muddy.

The footballers were furious. Their match was ruined.

Jake couldn't understand why everybody was so upset. Surely, they'd had a lovely time. A good chase and all that mud. But even Sam was cross with him, and he was led home in disgrace.

Chapter Three

Sam couldn't stay cross with Jake for long. Jake looked so upset at not being friends that the next day, Sam and Jake went to the park as usual.

Today, the park was quite deserted except

for a couple of shifty-looking boys. They seemed to be on the look out for trouble. They watched as Sam put Jake through his paces.

"O.K. Jake. It's nice and quiet today. Let's go!" Sam kicked the ball high into the air. Jake waited in just the right spot for the ball to come down and before it touched the ground, he bounced it off his muzzle, not once, but three times! Then he dribbled the ball back to Sam, and placed it right at Sam's feet.

Sam gave the ball another mighty kick. Jake rushed away after it, but at that moment, one of the watching boys stepped forward and caught the ball. Then he pulled something from his pocket. It was long, shiny and very sharp. It was a knife! The boy stabbed the ball. The ball instantly burst.

"Won't be able to do your tricks now!" he sneered and he kicked out at Jake.

Sam wasn't bothered about the ball but seeing this thug kick out at Jake made his blood boil. He marched up to the boy and took him by the scruff of the neck. The boy was so taken aback that he dropped his knife.

"Now then, you bully, you pick on someone your own size and leave a dumb animal alone," said Sam.

He let go of the boy and, shaking, put Jake on his lead and took him home.

When Jake and Sam arrived back at Jake's house, Jake's owner answered the door.

"My goodness, are you all right, Mr Haagen? You look so pale! It wasn't Jake, was it? Was he a bad boy again?" Mrs Foster asked.

"No, no, he's never a bad dog. No, it was nothing, it's all sorted out."

"Would you like a cup of tea?" asked Mrs Foster.

"No thank you."

Really Sam would have liked a cup of tea but he was too shy to accept.

When Sam had gone home, Jake had his

dinner then a nap. When he woke up he went out into the garden to see Holly.

Excitedly he told his friend all that had happened in the park.

Holly was anxious to know if Jake was all right. She was worried about Sam as well but Jake told her that Sam had been wonderful, a real hero. He added that, if he had had the chance, he would have seen the boys off. Holly smiled. Jake liked to boast about what he could do. Holly often wondered what he really could do!

Holly could hear her owner calling her in for the night, so she gave Jake a friendly nuzzle through the fence and left him on his own.

Jake strolled around his garden for a little while, checking up on things. When he reached the hole into Sam's garden, he thought he'd just pop through to check out the frogs. They were always very lively at this time of night.

As Jake reached the pond, he was surprised to hear the sound of shouting. It seemed to be coming from the direction of Sam's back door.

Jake didn't like the shouting. He sensed that something was wrong.

He rushed towards the back door, then saw a horrible sight. Two boys were pushing Sam backwards and forwards between them. They were pushing harder and harder. Sam was shouting at them to stop but this just made them push even more. They pushed Sam so hard that he fell to the ground.

Horrified, Jake saw one of the boys take something from his pocket. Jake's hackles rose. He remembered the burst football.

These thugs were the boys from the park. They'd come to get their own back on Sam. But they had reckoned without Jake.

With a ferocious snarl, Jake flew at the boy with the knife and grabbed his arm in his powerful jaws, forcing him to the ground. The boys were totally taken by surprise. The one on the ground was helpless. Jake pinned him down hard. The other one started kicking at Jake, trying to make him let go.

The kicks hurt Jake dreadfully. He yelped, but he would not let go. He knew it was the only chance Sam had to get help. Sam picked himself up and stumbled into the house to telephone the police. At that moment, the thug who was kicking at Jake decided to run for it.

When Sam came back, the boy with the knife was still on the ground with Jake on top of him, his long muzzle pushed into the boy's face. Jake held the boy down with his legs. He snarled at the boy if he tried to move. Jake seemed like a different dog from the one who'd played football in the park. His claws were very sharp, his teeth looked deadly and his eyes menacing.

The police seemed to be a very long time and Sam began to wonder if they would ever come. But Jake didn't move. He held the boy down the whole time. When the police arrived, two of them rushed in and grabbed the boy on the ground. Only then did Jake let go.

"Well, well, look who it is," said one of the policeman. "It's Eddie Price. Well done, dog. You've caught a very nasty villain! Last week, these two boys hurt an old lady so badly that she's still recovering in hospital. Bullies, that's what they are. Thanks to this dog, *he* won't be bullying anybody else and we'll soon find his pal."

Sam rushed over to Jake to see if he was all right. Jake felt very sore and bruised from the kicking and, in particular, his right back leg felt very stiff.

The neighbours had heard the sound of the police cars arriving. Most had rushed out into the street, others were peering through the curtains. Soon, it seemed that half the street was arriving in Sam's garden, including Jake's owners and Holly. As the story of what had happened became clear, everyone agreed that the hero of the day was Jake.

"What a marvellous dog!" they said.

"What a brave dog! Saved Sam's life, I don't doubt."

"Always knew he was an unusual dog!"

Jake couldn't really understand why they were making so much fuss. He loved Sam and he couldn't bear to see him hurt. It was as simple as that. Still, it was rather nice to be told that he had done something right for a change!

Chapter Four

In the days following the attack on Sam, Jake became quite a celebrity. The local newspaper sent a reporter to interview Sam and Jake's owners.

At first, Sam wasn't very keen on this because it meant that he had to speak. Jake's owners helped him and gradually Sam actually began to enjoy talking to people. He found he knew more English than he thought. A new friendship developed between the Foster family and their neighbour Sam.

As for Jake, he loved every minute of it. He always enjoyed attention and he posed happily for the newspaper photographer who thought that Jake was a perfect model. He had taken quite a few pictures in the garden when suddenly, Jake pricked up his ears. He'd heard the sound of the washing machine door being opened. While Mr Foster was busy talking to the photographer, Jake sneaked off into the house to help sort out the dirty washing.

After a while, Mr Foster and the photographer noticed that Jake had disappeared.

"Come on, Jake! Here boy!" Mr Foster called. "We just need a couple more."

Jake's head appeared round the corner of the back door with a pair of Mr Foster's underpants wrapped around it. That very second, the photographer's camera flashed. Next morning, Jake appeared in the newspapers wearing a rather unusual hat!

Mrs Foster read out the newspaper headline over breakfast.

"Wonder dog tames attacker," she said proudly. "That's our Jake!" and she chuckled at the photograph.

Holly was thrilled. At last her friend was receiving the attention she thought he deserved. She told Jake that she was very proud of him. He was quite right, he had indeed 'seen them off'! She'd seen his picture on the front page of the newspapers.

Jake pretended that he thought everybody was making a big fuss. But secretly he was very pleased to suddenly be so popular.

There was one thing, though, that did bother Jake. His leg, which had been so cruelly kicked by the thug, was still very stiff. He couldn't walk without limping.

The day after the attack, he was taken to the vets, which he hated. He always hated the vets. He hated the smells and he hated having to sit on that table. He didn't hate the vet though, who seemed quite nice. The vet gave Jake a thorough examination.

"Well, Mrs Foster, I don't think Jake has come to any real harm from his brave ordeal. I'm not so sure about this leg though. I think it's dislocated and although it will heal, he may be left with a limp."

Jake didn't like that idea. He liked to be

able to charge about everywhere and a limp would really slow him down. "Well," he thought. "It was a small price to pay to save Sam from being hurt."

Next day, Charles, the Irish Wolfhound, began to take Jake in hand. Charles went up to Jake now and gave him a friendly nudge with his huge head.

Charles realised that his old father had been wrong. He was forced to admit that it

didn't matter what a dog looked like. It was
how he behaved that counted.

Holly stood by and beamed at the pair of
them. She didn't like it when people weren't
friendly to one another so she was thrilled
to see Charles accepting Jake at last.

Charles decided to teach Jake to march
properly, like his old father. He was sure
Jake's limp would not seem half so bad.
Charles assured Jake that he would have

him fit for duty in any army in no time!

And so daily lessons with Charles, the gentle giant, began, with tips from Holly.

The first lesson Jake learned from Charles was how to stand smartly to attention. Charles stood proudly, chest out, head held high, legs straight and tail down. Jake tried to copy him.

Holly called out from her garden that this was how she had to stand in the show ring, and Charles agreed.

Charles began to show Jake how to place his feet slowly and deliberately, two legs at a time, on opposite sides, so that they moved in perfect harmony. Holly thought what a comical couple they made: the proud Charles striding out and the limping Jake following behind as best he could. But she didn't laugh, not so much as a titter. She wouldn't have dreamed of hurting their feelings.

After the first lesson, Jake crawled through the fence to Sam's garden.

Sam was feeding his birds, so Jake waited quietly.

"Hallo boy, how's your poor old leg? Come here, let Sam rub it for you," and Sam soothed Jake's injured leg, and made it feel easier. "When your leg is better Jake, we'll go to the park again. I've got a new ball."

Jake nuzzled at Sam's hand. He was quiet and not his boisterous self. He wondered if his leg would ever get better. He hoped so.

Chapter Five

After some time, the fuss over Jake died down. Jake began to get used to the shorter and colder days as autumn gave way to winter. The vet gave permission for Jake to be taken for his walks again. The weather was not very good, so Sam only took him out occasionally and Jake's footballing skills were becoming a little rusty. And he still had a slight limp.

One day, Jake squeezed through the hedge into Sam's garden and barked outside Sam's door to let him know he had arrived. Sam let him into the kitchen. To Jake's surprise, instead of the usual welcome dog biscuit, Sam gave him one of his own special shortbread biscuits.

"I shouldn't really give you this, Jakie, but I think you deserve it today," said Sam. "In my paper, it says they've put those two thugs in prison for a good long time. The poor old lady they attacked is in hospital." Sam thought for a moment. "They could have done the same to me if it hadn't been for you," he said, and he hugged Jake.

The pair of them went to the park and although Jake was a little slower, he still played football.

As Jake was dribbling the ball back to Sam, he found a rather nice patch of fox's dung and so he decided to roll in it. To his surprise Sam shouted at him to stop. "Not today, Jake. Got to smell your best!"

Jake wondered what Sam meant. He didn't usually stop him rolling. Besides, if he needed to smell his best, surely he had better carry on rolling! But he didn't. He always tried to do what Sam said.

When Jake and Sam arrived at Jake's house, Mrs Foster had a cup of tea waiting for Sam. Sam always had a cup of tea with her these days.

Jake was pleased. He wanted Sam to see where he slept. He was very proud of his present cardboard box. Jake's owners had once bought him a proper dog basket but he'd never slept in it, preferring to stick to his cardboard box. So they had given up and now they just kept replacing the boxes. He'd been working on this one since it

arrived as a replacement for his last one and he felt it was now just about perfect. Of course, it wouldn't stay like that, they never did. They seemed to quickly lose their shape.

Today Sam wasn't paying attention. "I tried to stop him rolling, Mrs Foster, but you know what he is," he said.

"Oh, don't worry, Sam. I'm going to sort him out later," replied Mrs Foster.

"Well, I'll be going then. See you soon. Bye Jake, see you boy."

Jake was worried. What did Mrs Foster mean when she said, "I'm going to sort him out later?" It didn't sound too good. It sounded horribly like a bath was on its way. Jake decided that he'd better lie low. For the rest of the day, Jake stayed out of the way, in case he was right.

That night, Jake heard the sound he dreaded – the sound of the bath water running. And he could smell that awful stuff they put in the water. As soon as he saw Mrs Foster's plastic apron, he knew the worst was about to happen. He was to be bathed.

How could they do it? It had taken him ages to work up the smell he had now and he was particularly pleased with it. Weeks of work washed down the plug hole in minutes!

"Besides," thought Jake, "it's crazy in this weather. It's freezing cold."

Straightaway, Jake put his bath plan into action. He followed this whenever he was threatened with a bath. His aim was to make life as difficult as possible for the person giving him the bath.

First, Jake made himself scarce. If Mrs Foster couldn't find him then she couldn't bath him.

This time, when Mrs Foster tracked him down, she found him squeezed under the spare bed. Jake hadn't hidden there since he was a puppy. When he tried to get out, he remembered *why*. It was really much too small for him now. Mrs Foster had to lift the bed up to get him out.

If he couldn't actually avoid being put into the bath, the second part of Jake's bath plan was never to keep still whilst in the water. First he sat down, then he jumped

up and turned himself round and round and round until he made himself dizzy. After that he had to keep still, and so Mrs Foster managed to clean him up.

Finally, Jake would try to make as much mess as he could when he stepped out of the bath. If he was wet, then he made sure everybody else got wet too. This time, he shook himself before Mrs Foster could get the towel on him. He soaked her, the floor, the walls and all the dry towels hanging by the bath.

"That was a good one!" thought Jake. "I won!"

He expected to be scolded and he was surprised that Mrs Foster wasn't more cross. She only told him off lightly. Jake was actually a bit disappointed.

"This is odd," thought Jake. "A bath in mid-winter, a thorough soaking and all she says is 'Oh Jake'. There's something funny going on."

After his bath, Jake was given his supper and allowed to lie in front of the fire to dry off. As he went to sleep that night, he actually felt rather comfortable. He had to admit to himself that perhaps, just occasionally, a bath wasn't so bad after all.

Just occasionally, mind.

Chapter Six

The following day, Jake was surprised to find everybody up and about before he was properly awake. It was still dark. Jake climbed out of his box and stretched his early morning stretch. He trotted up to greet Mrs Foster, as usual, as she entered the kitchen, only to get another surprise.

Mrs Foster was already dressed and wearing clothes that Jake had only seen her wear on special occasions.

"Morning, Jakie. Oh good, you still look

smart. Come here, let's give you a final brush up."

"A final brush up! You're joking!" thought Jake.

Although he had been taken by surprise and was still a bit dozy, Jake immediately fell to the floor and lay down, flat out. As he lay there, Mrs Foster brushed what she could. Eventually and rather reluctantly, Jake stood up for her.

"What is this all about?" thought Jake. "Oh, I know. We're going to visit her mother. She doesn't like me much. She doesn't like the way I smell. I hope it's not for long. I'd better say goodbye to Holly and Sam before we go. I hope they're up."

After the grooming, Jake was allowed out into the garden for some last minute checks. To his surprise, everything was quiet next door in Holly's garden. Sam was not about either, but it was a bit early for him. Jake heard his owners calling and he knew that this meant the beginning of a long boring journey.

Jake jumped into the car and prepared himself for several sleeps. He was surprised to see that even Mr Foster was all dressed up. He looked rather uncomfortable in his suit.

Jake was right. The journey lasted about five sleeps. A long one. That meant no more walks with Sam for a while.

At long last, as the car began to slow down, Jake sat up to see what was happening. The car was pulling into a great big concrete car park. There were lots of other cars there, many of them with pictures of dogs on them.

"Well, this is odd," thought Jake. "Are we stopping for a drink?"

Mr and Mrs Foster got out of the car but there were no drinks in sight. Jake had his lead put on and he jumped out.

"I think this is the way," said Mrs Foster. "Anyway, I've got the passes, so we can go in anywhere."

Jake trotted along beside them, feeling more and more puzzled.

After they'd walked for five minutes, Jake saw a very large building looming up in front of them. He couldn't understand the writing on it but it seemed like an important building. When they reached one of the side doors, Mrs Foster handed some pieces of paper to a man.

"Oh good, I'm so glad you've made it. So pleased to meet you at last."

"I think he means me," thought Jake.

When Jake stepped inside the building, he knew where he was at once.

He had dreamed about it so much.

He was at Crufts.

Crufts! He could hardly believe it.

He took a deep breath and smelt all the

delicious smells. It was just as Holly had described it. The banners. The big green carpets. But most of all, the dogs!

Everywhere he looked there were dogs. Tall dogs, small dogs, some very hairy dogs, others nearly bald! Some dogs barked excitedly to each other, whilst others sat patiently on wooden benches. In his whole life, Jake had never seen so many dogs. He stood gazing at everything around him with a wonderful expression of contentment on his face.

So, this was Crufts. At last!

A man with a badge came to meet Jake and his owners. He took them to have a cup of tea and some biscuits and a drink of water for Jake.

"Now, I expect you would like to have a look round first, wouldn't you?" said the

Crufts man. "That's fine, but please make sure you're back here in time."

So off they went for a good look around.

Jake met the dogs that pulled sledges. They were called Alaskan Malamutes.

He talked with some dogs called Great Danes who were nearly as big as Charles, and he met some Chihuahuas from Mexico that were so small that he nearly trod on one!

Jake had been talking to one dog for nearly five minutes before he realised he was talking to its tail, not its head!

Some dogs had such fancy haircuts that Jake thought they looked more like hedges than dogs.

Jake met the Belgian Shepherd dogs. These, he thought, were the most handsome of all the dogs. Perhaps because they looked a bit like him.

"Just like my grandad!" he thought.

As Jake walked amongst the food stalls, he was given so many tit-bits that even he began to feel full.

Everybody seemed to know who he was and wanted to make a fuss of him. Jake thought it was wonderful.

Eventually, the Fosters and Jake arrived back where they had started.

The Crufts man was waiting for them.

"Right," he said, "here's somebody I think you know. He's been having lunch with us," and to Jake's surprise and joy, there was Sam, standing in front of him!

Sam was wearing an outfit like Mr Foster's and he didn't smell like Sam at all. Obviously poor Sam had been forced to have a bath as well and have his hair combed. Jake jumped up at him and even though he was so dressed up, Sam didn't mind a bit.

"Jakie! Lovely to see you boy," said Sam.

"Well now, is everybody ready?" said the Crufts man briskly. "Then let's go."

Sam took Jake by the lead, and Jake found himself in a fenced off area with several other dogs.

"These other dogs will be coming in after you. We'd like Jake to lead our parade of heroes," the Crufts man said to Sam.

It was only then that Jake realised what

was about to happen. He was about to go into the Main Ring at Cruft's Dog Show!

Sam and Jake waited at the entrance to the ring, next to a large arrangement of flowers. Jake sniffed at the flowers and wrinkled his nose. He never could stand the smell of roses. He got up and moved towards them, but suddenly Sam was leading him into that great big green open space called the Main Ring!

All around the ring sat a huge crowd of people. As soon as they caught sight of Jake and Sam, they clapped and cheered.

Then a loud voice said, "And leading our parade is Jake, owned by Mr and Mrs Foster and accompanied by Mr Sam Haagen. Jake is to receive our award for exceptional bravery for saving Mr Haagen from a terribly violent attack."

Sam and Jake were joined in the middle of the big ring by a very important-looking lady. She beamed at Jake and patted his head. From a small table, she picked up a beautiful blue sash with silver edges and put it around Jake's neck.

She turned to Sam and handed him a silver medal with a ribbon which matched Jake's sash. Solemnly, they shook hands and paws, then Jake and Sam did a lap of honour around the ring. Again the people clapped and cheered. Jake was very glad that he'd had lessons from Charles. He stuck out his chest proudly as he trotted round. There was no sign of a limp.

Suddenly, Jake caught sight of Holly. She was standing over in a corner. As he passed, he couldn't resist stopping to talk to her. Holly told Jake her own marvellous news. She had been chosen as the best Rough Collie and would be in the big ring later!

"Wonderful!" thought Jake. "What a *wonderful* day!"

After their lap of honour, Jake and Sam were asked to stay in the centre whilst the other dogs in the parade came in.

There were five others. One dog had woken up his mistress when their house had caught fire. Another dog had sniffed out a haul of drugs that were being smuggled into the country in fake wine bottles. There was a police dog and next to him there was a Guide dog for the Blind who were both retiring after an exceptional number of years of faithful service. Another dog had stayed with his owner after he had injured himself in a climbing accident. The dog had kept him warm and alive until the rescuers arrived.

When all the dogs were in the ring, Jake and Sam were asked to lead a final parade of honour around the ring. Jake was at the front because he had risked his own life for Sam.

Jake had made it to Crufts after all. He wasn't a pedigree, and he could never match the dogs in the obedience competition. But there was one thing that Jake hadn't known. No one had told him about the special parade for exceptional dogs. Clever dogs. Brave dogs.

And Jake had proved himself the bravest of all.

Together, Sam and Jake left the ring. As they passed by the large flower arrangement, Jake caught the heavy perfume of the roses again.

"Pooh!" he thought. And he decided to do something about them.

Without warning, Jake went over to the arrangement, cocked his leg and watered the flowers.

A chorus of voices cried out . . .

"Oh Jake!"

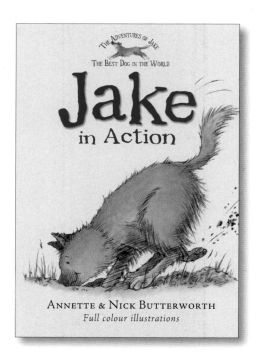

THE ADVENTURES OF JAKE

THE BEST DOG IN THE WORLD

Jake
in Action

ANNETTE & NICK BUTTERWORTH
Full colour illustrations

Jake is in disgrace – he's just dug up the roses.
And eaten something he shouldn't. But he usually
tries to be good – so that's why his friend Sam takes
him to the park for a game of football.

But their football pitch is threatened – the Council
want to sell Jake's park and build on it!

Everyone is determined to save the park, but it
seems their luck is out. Jake is a very special dog
– but can he save the day?